Toot & Puddle

The New Friend

by Holly Hobbie

LITTLE, BROWN AND COMPANY

New York ❧ Boston

Little, Brown and Company

Time Warner Book Group
1271 Avenue of the Americas, New York, NY 10020
Visit our Web site at www.lb-kids.com

First Edition

Library of Congress Cataloging-in-Publication Data

Hobbie, Holly.
    Toot & Puddle : the new friend / by Holly Hobbie. — 1st ed.
        p. cm.
    Summary: Opal's new friend Daphne seems to be the best at everything she does, but Toot
and Puddle see another side of her.
    ISBN 0-316-36636-6
    [1. Behavior—Fiction. 2. Friendship—Fiction. 3. Pigs—Fiction.] I. Title: Toot and Puddle.
II. Title

PZ7.H6517Ts 2004
[E]—dc22   2003054553

10 9 8 7 6 5 4 3 2 1

SC

Manufactured in China

The illustrations for this book were done in watercolor.
The text was set in Optima, and the display type was set in Windsor Light.

On a sunny day in October, Opal came to Woodcock Pocket for a visit, and she brought along her new friend, Daphne.

"Isn't Daphne beautiful?" Opal said.

"She's quite pretty," said Puddle, smiling at the new friend.

Daphne did perfect cartwheels.

She could stand on her head perfectly. And she could do a back flip.

"You certainly are talented," Toot told her. "I'll never be that good at gymnastics," said Opal.

"No one jumps rope better than Daphne,"
said Opal.
"Faster!" cried Daphne. "Faster!"

"What shall we do for fun tonight?" Puddle asked.

"I know," Toot said. "Let's see who can stand on one leg the longest."

"One, two, three, go!" Daphne cried excitedly.

Toot wobbled and soon tipped over.
Opal plunked flat on her bottom.
Finally, Puddle lost his balance, too.
The last one standing
         on one leg
            was Daphne.

"Let's see who can hold their breath the longest," Puddle suggested next.

"One, two, three, go!" shouted Daphne.

Puddle was the first to give up this time. Then Opal. And finally even Toot. The last one left holding her breath was little Daphne.

"I don't know how you do it," Puddle said.

"It's easy," Daphne said. "I just do it."

For the evening's entertainment, Opal performed bird songs. She imitated an owl and a crow and a duck. *Hoo, Hoo,* she went. *Caw, caw. Quack, quack, quack.*

Toot and Puddle clapped and whistled.

"Can you do the nightingale?" Daphne asked. "That's my favorite."

But Opal didn't know the nightingale's song.

When it was Daphne's turn to perform, she played a Mozart violin concerto perfectly.

"That was beautiful," said Opal.
"Lovely," Puddle agreed.
"Delightful," Toot chimed in.
"You certainly are musical."
Daphne took a bow.

"Sometimes I wish I was as good at things as Daphne is," said Opal.

"Everyone is different and everyone is good at different things," Puddle told her. "You're you. And Daphne is Daphne."

"But she's better at everything," said Opal.

In the morning, Opal and Daphne drew pictures of themselves with crayons, and they asked Toot and Puddle to be art judges. Who made the best self-portrait?

"Hmm," Puddle said. "They're just completely different."

"They are," Toot agreed. "Opal's picture is more realistic, and Daphne's is less realistic."

"I know," Daphne said. "I like less realistic."

After lunch, everyone played Go Fish, which was Opal's favorite card game. She won three times in a row.

"Hooray!" she cheered. "It's my lucky day."

"I'm bored," Daphne said. "I quit."

For supper, Puddle made noodles with his favorite homemade dandelion sauce.

But Daphne said, "I don't like dandelion sauce."

"Puddle makes the best," said Opal.

"Just try one bite," Toot coaxed.

"I want mine plain," Daphne insisted.

"I think your new friend is a bit of a prima donna," Toot said.

"What's a prima donna?" Opal asked.

"Someone who thinks she is overly special," Puddle explained. "Like the biggest shooting star in the sky."

"Well, I think Daphne *is* overly special," was Opal's reply.

But in the morning, Daphne refused to eat Toot's delicious oatmeal. "I never have oatmeal," she huffed. "I usually have pancakes with maple syrup."

Later, the new friend refused to help rake leaves, even for a little while.

"Come on, Daphne," Puddle called. "Raking leaves is piles of fun."

"I can't," Daphne said. "I might get a blister."

"Maybe you are a prima donna," Opal said. Her pink face flushed pinker.

"What's that?" Daphne asked. "I never heard of it."

"It's someone who thinks she is so special she won't even help rake leaves."

"Well, maybe someone just doesn't like to get blisters," Daphne said, "because they sting like mad—especially if she needs to practice violin."

Everyone was enjoying the quiet end of the day when a scary, high-pitched squeal filled the house.

"Where is Daphne?" Puddle asked anxiously.

"She went to take a bubble bath," Opal told him.

Toot was the first one out of his chair.

"Look!" Daphne cried, shivering. "A creepy-crawly."

"Holy moly!" Puddle shouted. "That's a big one."

"Nothing to fear," Toot declared.

"I'm scared," said Daphne in a small, shaky voice. She was on the brink of tears. "I'm really scared."

But Opal seemed positively thrilled. "I'm sure this is a friendly spider, Daphne. And what a big, beautiful spider you are," she said excitedly.

After Opal had coaxed the creepy-crawly into a glass jar, she took it outside to the woodpile.

"I hope you enjoy your new home, Mr. Spider. Bye-bye."

"You were so brave with that spider," Daphne said. "I wish I could be that brave."

"I bet you could be," said Opal.

"No," Daphne said. "Spiders give me goose bumps."

"But don't you like spider webs?" Opal asked. "Spiders are the only thing that can make them."

Daphne had to admit she had never seen a spider web.

"You have to be on the lookout to spot one," Opal told her. "Wait until you do." Then she turned out the bedroom light. "Are you ready to go to sleep?"

"I have an idea," Daphne said. "Let's see who can fall asleep the fastest. One, two, three, go!"

In no time, Daphne was sound asleep. Her contented snoring sounded like the purr of a cat. Opal, however, wasn't ready to go to sleep yet. She wanted to stay awake and gaze at the night sky, as she often did when she came to Woodcock Pocket. There was always something to see.